MR. GOOD

originated by Roger Hargreaves

Written and illustrated by
Adam Hargreaves

PSS!
PRICE STERN SLOAN
An Imprint of Penguin Group (USA) Inc.

Mr. Good is very good.

He always makes his bed.
He always brushes his teeth.
And he always wipes his feet.

He never slams doors.
He never forgets birthdays.
And he never, ever tells lies.

Mr. Good is very, very good.

However, Mr. Good lives in a place called Badland.

A place where nobody is like Mr. Good.

A place where people do slam doors.

And they slam them in your face!

In Badland, the puddles are much deeper than they look.

In Badland, a dog's bite is worse than its bark.

In Badland, even the trees are bad!

One day it was wet and windy.

Well, of course it was.

The weather is always bad in Badland.

Mr. Good was walking along, minding his own business, when the hat of the man in front of him blew off.

Mr. Good leapt in the air and caught it for him.

The man turned around and glared at Mr. Good.

"What do you think you're doing?" he thundered. "Give my hat back!"

Poor Mr. Good.

This sort of thing was always happening to him.

You see, the very idea of doing a good deed in Badland was preposterous, unthinkable, mad.

If Mr. Good offered to help carry shopping, he was accused of stealing.

If he kindly held a door open for someone,
then he would be kicked in the shin!

Not surprisingly, Mr. Good was not very happy.

In fact, he was miserable.

So he decided to go for a long walk to think about things.

He walked for a very long time.

He was so deep in thought that he did not notice how far he had gone.

And he was so deep in thought that he accidentally walked slap-bang into somebody.

"Oh . . . oh . . . I . . . I . . . I'm s-s-so s-s-sorry," stammered Mr. Good nervously.

"That's quite all right," said the man, and carried on his way.

"Quite all right," repeated Mr. Good to himself. "That's quite all right?"

In the whole of his life, no one had ever said "that's quite all right" to Mr. Good.

Then Mr. Good noticed that the sun was shining.

Which was strange, because the sun never shone in Badland.

Farther on, Mr. Good found a trash can on its side.

Without thinking, he tidied up all the trash.

"Thank you," said a woman.

Mr. Good stared at her.

In the whole of his life, no one had ever said "thank you" to him.

"Could you tell me where I am?" he asked.

"You're in Goodland," replied the woman.

"Thank you," said Mr. Good.

"My pleasure," said the woman.

Mr. Good beamed.

And I am sure you have guessed that Mr. Good now lives in Goodland.

And Mr. Good is happy.

Very, very happy doing good deeds all day long.

The only thing Mr. Good still does not trust are puddles.

Once you have stepped in a Badland puddle,
you never forget!